The High Flying Adventures of Aaron the Airplane!

MICHAEL P. YOURCHISIN

PAGE PUBLISHING, INC.
Conneaut Lake, PA

First originally published by Page Publishing 2021

ISBN 978-1-6624-4615-3 (hc)
ISBN 978-1-6624-4616-0 (digital)

Printed in the United States of America

To my three children and the newest member of the family, grandson Ozzie.

A Special Note for Parents Before Reading *The High Flying Adventures of Aaron the Airplane!* with Your Child

Reading a story is easy. Reading a familiar story is easy, predictable, but potentially boring. Reading a story that is familiar but changes with your child's interests and activities becomes that comforting, snuggling, feel-good finish to a day that helps children nod off in your arms or while lying in bed that puts a warm glow in us all.

The High Flying Adventures of Aaron the Airplane! can be that story. His colors can change to any that suit you or your child (or children)! The activities that Aaron sees are whatever your child has been doing—playing in the park, soccer, riding bikes, running, skipping, walking, indoors or outdoors, or even moping around the house.

Aaron's adventures allow him to soar above all while he comments about all that he sees and what your child shares concerning what occurred that day.

The sharing of the day's events becomes an inclusive activity between Aaron, children, grandparents, and parents even when adult jobs and commitments preclude both parents from being as involved in the day as you might have wished.

Everything about Aaron's story is changeable—time, place, colors, weather, activity of the day, you call the shots. The story is all yours to embellish and to create the world that best suits you and your child.

And now a basic Aaron the Airplane story that worked for my kids, having three children (twins 22 months after our firstborn), Aaron sometimes flew three different times a night as each child got their special personal Aaron the Airplane bedtime story. Enjoy!

Once upon a time…

There was a fine old…

Neat old…

Superold plane by the name of…

Aaron the Airplane!

He has big blue wings, a tiny
red tail, and a very shiny silver
propeller.

And one fine day, he got ready to see what adventures he could find.

Brrrm, brrrm, brrrm! He sputtered as he flew up, up, up into the skyway high in the air.

He flew and flew and flew until he found...

You!

17

And what did Aaron find out about you today? Were you outside playing? Aaron loves to see children playing!

Note to parents: Now you can either make up a story of Aaron seeing activities zooming up and down as you tickle and laugh together, or your child can share with you and Aaron what they did today.

What would you like to tell Aaron about your day? Aaron loves to hear stories!

Well, it's time for Aaron to take off again…

Brrrm, brrrm, brrrm! It's up, up, up higher and higher to visit the other children in the neighborhood.

So until the next time Aaron comes to visit, good night, sleep tight, and I'll see you on my next flight!

The End

27

CPSIA information can be obtained
at www.ICGtesting.com
Printed in the USA
LVHW071135310122
709436LV00028B/228